T0365427

Three Little Birds Flew Away

Marilyn Sandberg Grenat

Three Little Birds Flew Away

iUniverse books may be ordered through booksellers or by contacting:

iUniverse
1663 Liberty Drive
Bloomington, IN 47403
www.iuniverse.com
844-349-9409

Because of the dynamic nature of the Internet, any web addresses or links contained in this book may have changed since publication and may no longer be valid. The views expressed in this work are solely those of the author and do not necessarily reflect the views of the publisher, and the publisher hereby disclaims any responsibility for them.

Any people depicted in stock imagery provided by Getty Images are models,
and such images are being used for illustrative purposes only.
Certain stock imagery © Getty Images.

ISBN: 978-1-6632-6401-5 (sc)
978-1-6632-6402-2 (hc)
978-1-6632-6400-8 (e)

Library of Congress Control Number: 2024912490

Print information available on the last page.

iUniverse rev. date: 06/26/2024

Dedication

Harrison Cohen and I, his Momo, Marilyn Sandberg Grenat, would like to dedicate this book, "Three Little Birds Flew Away" to his little sister, Charlotte Cohen, his cousins, Sylvia Zanker, Marlee and River Patrick, his mommy Kelsey and daddy Brett Cohen and his grandparents. Harry worked real hard on getting all his pictures together for our book.

One cold spring day

Momo looked out her
window only to see,

Three little birds sitting high in the tree.

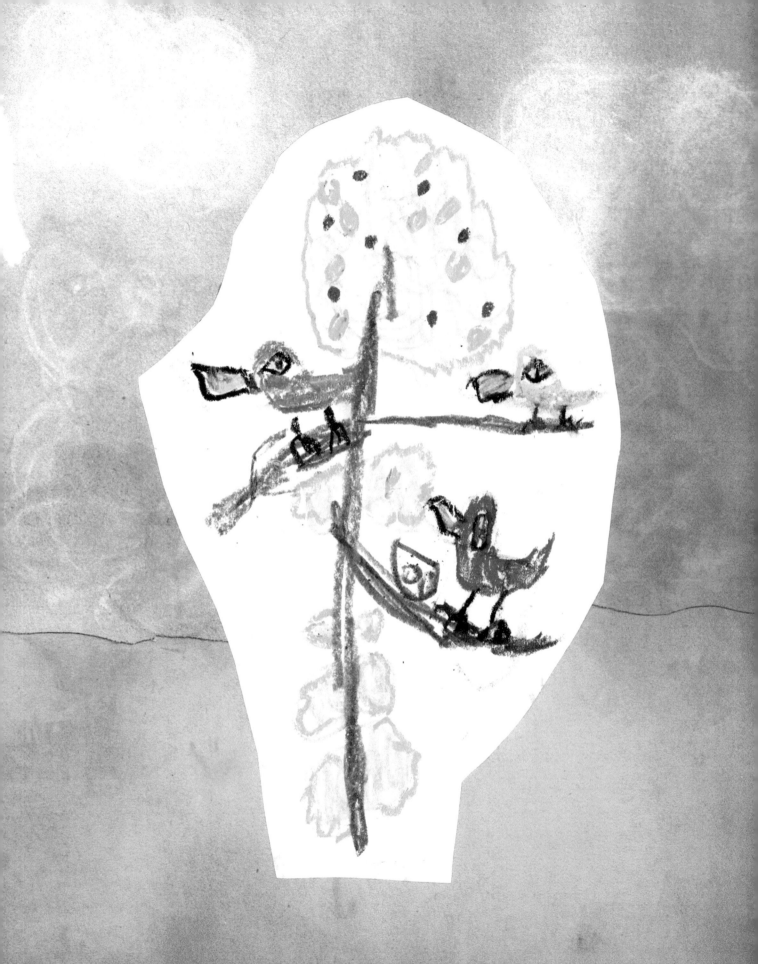

They were surveying their surroundings,

Hoping the wind and rain wouldn't
be giving them a pounding.

3

One, two, three little birdies way up high,

Sittin' on a branch in the sky.

They looked so alone,

That I worried they out of
the tree may be blown.

The rain had brought the creatures out,

But now they realized they
needed to spread about.

They watched as the little bugs
and worms crawled to safety,

But 'Oh' they thought,
'They would be so tasty!'

They watched and started to sing,

Until soon they decided to
upon them spring!

The soft earth allowed
them to scurry away,

And then they planned another
day to come out and play.

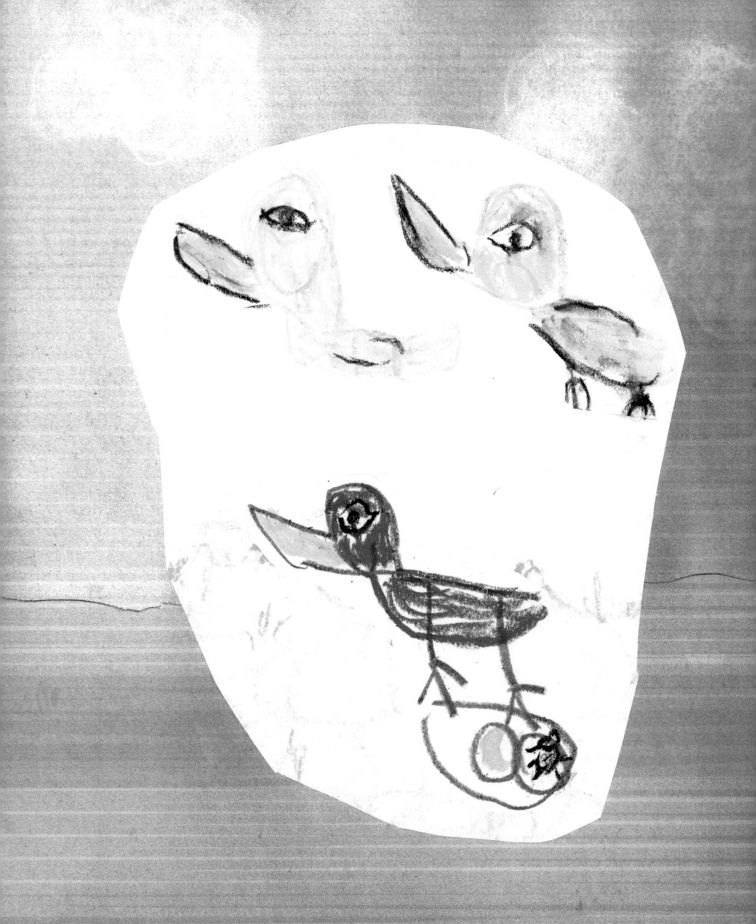

So the three little birds flew away!

No creatures for them today!

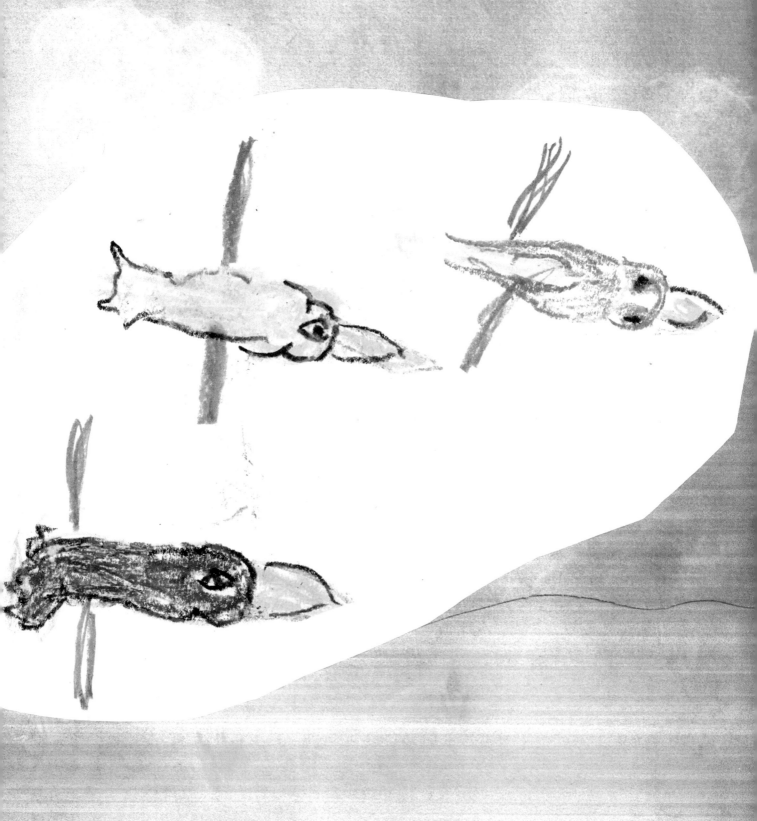

Printed in the United States
by Baker & Taylor Publisher Services

This is the fourth book that Marilyn Sandberg Grenat has completed with a similar genre of poetry, which was her first book. However, this is a completely different project in that it is a children's book. This being combined with her five year old great grandson, Harrison Cohen's illustrations. It has been exciting for both of them to do this together.

* * * * *

Marilyn Sandberg Grenat is a mother, grandmother, and a great grandmother, and her family, and many friends, call her "Momo", which is short for mother's mother in "Swedish". She lives in Lafayette, Indiana and her great Grandson lives in Carmel, Indiana. He just recently graduated from daycare and will be attending Kindergarten in the Fall. He lives with his Mother and Dad and little sister, Charlotte. Momo feels he is very talented with his drawings, so we were anxious to do this project together. Thank you Harry for all your help.

Author - Marilyn Sandberg Grenat

Illustrator - Harrison Cohen, 5 years old

U.S. $14.99

ISBN 978-1-6632-6401-5
51499

9 781663 264015

iUniverse®
www.iuniverse.com